CAMILLE

CAMILLE:
A PLAY IN FIVE ACTS

Alexander Dumas, Jr.

Translated By

Matilda Heron

AYER COMPANY, PUBLISHERS, INC.
SALEM, NEW HAMPSHIRE 03079

First Published 1856
Reprinted 1975

Reprint Edition 1985
AYER Company, Publishing, Inc.
382 Main Street
Salem, New Hampshire 03079

INTERNATIONAL STANDARD BOOK NUMBER:
0-8369-8887-6

LIBRARY OF CONGRESS CATALOG CARD NUMBER:
76-170697

PRINTED IN THE UNITED STATES OF AMERICA

CAMILLE:

A

PLAY IN FIVE ACTS:

TRANSLATED FROM THE FRENCH OF ALEXANDER DUMAS, JR.,

BY

MATILDA HERON,

WHILE IN PARIS.

———•◦•———

AYER COMPANY, PUBLISHERS, INC.
SALEM, NEW HAMPSHIRE 03079

CHARACTERS IN THE PLAY.

ARMAND DUVAL.
MONSIEUR DUVAL, Father of Armand.
COUNT DE VARVILLE.
GASTON.
GUSTAVE.
MESSENGER.

CAMILLE.
PRUDENCE.
OLIMPE.
NICHETTE.
NANINE.

CAMILLE.

ACT FIRST.

SCENE:—*A room in the house of Camille.*

COUNT DE VARVILLE AND NANINE DISCOVERED.

Door-bell rings as the curtain rises.

Varville. Some one has rung the bell.

Nanine. Yes, I hear. Valentine will attend to the door.

Varville. Perhaps it is Camille.

Nanine. No, not yet. She said she would return at half-past ten, and it is not ten yet. [*Nichette speaks without.*] Ah, it is Mademoiselle Nichette's voice.

Nichette. [ENTERING.] Oh, excuse me! I thought Mademoiselle Camille was here.

Nanine. No, Nichette, she is not in. Do you wish to see her?

Nichette. I was merely passing the door, and I felt like coming up to say good-night to her. But since she is not here, you will please tell her that I called.

Nanine. Will you wait awhile? She will soon be in.

Nichette. No, thank you! Gustave is at the door. Is she well?

Nanine. Ah,—always the same.

Nichette. Did she leave with you the little bundle that I requested of her the other day?

Nanine. Yes; but you are not going to carry it?

Nichette. Why not? It is not heavy.

Nanine. You had better let me send it to you, and save you the trouble.

Nichette. I thank you. But nothing is a trouble that I do for Camille. Please tell her that I will do these very nicely, and bring them to her in a few days, and that I left my love for her. Adieu, Nanine! Adieu, Monsieur! [EXIT.

Varville. Umph! A very pretty girl! Who is she?

Nanine. That is Mademoiselle Nichette.

Varville. Nichette! That's the name of a cat, not a woman.

Nanine. It is a pet name that Camille gave her. They are very fond of each other. They used to be companions, and worked together in the same room.

Varville. What! Worked? Did Camille ever work?

Nanine. Yes—she was an embroidress.

Varville. Why, I never knew that before.

Nanine. It was your own fault, Monsieur; for Madam has made no secret of it.

Varville. This little puss—puss—what's her name? Ah! this *Nichette*, as you call her, is rather pretty.

Nanine. And more—she is *wise*.

Varville. Wise! Ah, yes,—well wise is a good word. But who is this Monsieur Gustave who was waiting for her below?

Nanine. He is her husband.

Varville. Oh, then he is Monsieur Nichette!

Nanine. That is, he is not her husband yet; but he will be, and that is the same thing.

Varville. I understand. She is wise as the world goes. But she has a lover.

Nanine. Who loves but her, and who will marry her, and make her a good husband. And take my word for it, she is a good girl, and deserves all the happiness he can bestow upon her.

Varville. So thrives every body's suit but mine. Nanine, do you think Camille cares any more for me than she used to? That is, do you think she really loves me?

Nanine. Not the least little bit in the world!

Varville. What? Pheugh! [*Aside.*] A strange way of answering a civil question that girl's got! [*To Nanine.*] But it must be said that she *has* strange taste, or she never could endure the tedious visits of that old Monsieur de Meuriac. They must be very annoying.

Nanine. You would not think so if you could hear how Madam speaks of him. Besides, poor old man, it is the only happiness he has, and he regards her as his own child.

Varville. Oh, yes! By the way, I heard of that very pathetic and interesting story; but unhappily I cannot believe it.

Nanine. Then listen to me, and I will endeavor to convince you. There are many evil things said of Madam, and with truth; but that is the very reason why things that are *not* true should not be said. About two years ago, Camille, after a long illness, determined to visit the celebrated waters of Bagneres, to recover, if possible, her health. I accompanied her. Among the invalids at the hotel there was a lovely young girl, the same age as Camille, suffering from the same complaint, and bearing such strong resemblance to her, that wherever they went, they were called the twin sisters. This young girl was Mademoiselle de Meuriac, daughter of the Duke.

Varville. Mademoiselle de Meuriac died.

Nanine. She did.

Varville. Oh, yes! I have heard this story before; and that the Duke implored Camille to change her course of life, promising that if she would consent to do so, he would charge himself with all her wants, and introduce her to society in which she would be loved and honored. Camille at length consented. This was not two years since; and to-night she is at the opera, the Queen of the Camelias, fifty thousand francs in debt.

Nanine. Which you have kindly offered to pay. Yes, you are right, Monsieur de Varville. Madam is gayer now than she ever was before; but no one knows her heart. Ah, sir, you would have pitied her had you seen her efforts to please the world in which the Duke de Meuriac sought to gain her a position. She was so gentle, so child-like, it seemed as if the spirit of the dead girl had left its innocence with her, and blotted out all record of the past. Day by day all who knew her grew to love her. But this was not to last. The Duke was called away. In his absence her story reached the circle in which she moved. From that moment it was closed against her. She was shunned as an adder; and in their cruel sneers they told her to go back to Paris and wear Camelias. She did return to Paris—met old friends, who gave a warmer welcome to her faults than the better world had given to her virtues. [*Door-bell rings.*] Ah, here she is! Shall I tell her what you were saying?

Varville. No, Nanine—you are too amiable to make mischief.

ENTER CAMILLE.

Camille. [*To Nanine.*] Order supper. Olimpe and Gaston will be here presently. I met them at the opera. [EXIT NANINE. *Seeing Varville.*] Ah, you are there!

Varville. Yes, it is my destiny to await you.

Camille. And it is my destiny to find you ever here on my return.

Varville. And it shall continue to be until you forbid me your door.

Camille. Indeed! am I never to enter this house without finding you here before me? What have you got to say, now that you are here?

Varville. You know the only subject of my heart.

Camille. Heart! I am sick of that.

Varville. Is it my fault if I love you too well?

Camille. There it is again! My good friend, if I were to listen to every man who tells me he loves me, I would not have time to breakfast. For the hundredth time, I repeat, Mon. de Varville, it will not do! You are losing time. You are ever welcome to enter here—when I go out, and to leave when I enter: but if you will insist on speaking to me of your love, you must not come at all.

Varville. A year ago, at Bagneres, Camille, you thought differently.

Camille. Yes; but that was a year ago. At Bagneres. A very dull place. I was sick. Things have changed. This is Paris. I am better now.

Varville. Especially since the Duke de Meuriac has adopted you.

Camille. You are a fool!

Varville. Or, perhaps, since the Count de Giray has been the chosen one.

Camille. Monsieur de Varville, I am at Liberty to love whom I please. That is purely my affair—certainly not yours. And if you have nothing else to say, go home. Good night. [*He goes up and sits at the fire. She goes to the piano and plays.*]

Varville. Bravo! Bravo!

Camille. Are you not gone yet?

Varville. No, not yet; I am waiting your better humor. [*She coughs.*] You are ill, Camille. What's the matter?

Camille. Nothing; I will be better—when you are gone.

Varville. Ah, I see my star is not propitious. So, I will say good night. Camille, shall I call to-morrow at one?

Camille. Yes, do. [*Aside.*] I shall be out from twelve till five.

Varville. Adieu. [*Goes up.*]

ENTER NANINE, *who announces Mademoiselle Olimpe and Monsieur Gaston, and* EXITS.—ENTER OLIMPE AND GASTON.

Camille. Come in, Olimpe, I thought you were never coming to see me any more.

Olimpe. It was all his fault.

Gaston. Yes, all my fault! It always is, you know. Ah, how are you, Varville?

Varville. How are you, Gaston? Glad to see you.

Gaston.   You sup with us to-night; do you not?

Varville.   Do I, Camille?

Camille.   No—no! Why, I thought you bid me good night just now.

Varville.   So I did; but I thought you called me back.

Gaston.   Well, my little girl, how have you been all this time?

Camille.   Oh, very well.

Gaston.   So much the better.   In passing the *Cafe de Paris*, I ordered some fine oysters and a basket of champagne of a certain brand, which they keep expressly for my use. It is excellent, I assure you!   So *vive la joi!*—there will be no scarcity of amusement.

Olimpe.   There never is when you are about.

Gaston.   Mademoiselle Olimpe, you are a wicked woman.

Olimpe.   No wonder, I keep bad company.   [*To Camille.*] Will Prudence be here?

Camille.   Yes, she should be here by this time.   [*Calls at window.*]   Prudence.

Olimpe.   Oh, Prudence is your neighbor, is she?

Camille.   Yes, she lives just opposite.   It is very convenient.   When I want her, I have only to open the window and call.   [*Calls.*]   Prudence!

Gaston.   Who is Madame Prudence?

Olimpe.   She is a milliner, and has but one customer,— Camille.

Gaston.   What, Camille, do you wear all her bonnets?

Camille.   Oh, no,—heaven forbid!   It is bad enough to have to pay for them.   But she is a good soul, with a heart as light as her purse.   [*Calls.*]   Prudence!

Prudence.   [*Without.*]   Here I am.

Camille.   Well, here we are waiting for you.   Why do you not come?

Prudence.   I cannot just now.

Camille.   What detains you?

Prudence.   A young man whom I have not seen for a long

time has just stepped in to see me, and I cannot leave him alone.

Camille. Then bring him along. Quick! Quick! Ugh! how cold it is! Mon. de Varville, do pray, put some wood on that fire, I am frozen here. Make yourself useful, for you are not agreeable. [*Varville fixes fire.*]

ENTER NANINE, *who announces Monsieur Armand Duval and Madam Duverney.*

Camille. Bid them enter. [EXIT NANINE.

ENTER ARMAND AND PRUDENCE.

Prudence. My dear Camille, allow me to present to you Monsieur Armand Duval.

Camille. Must I rise?

Armand. No Madam; it is not necessary. [*Goes and speaks to others.*]

Camille. [*To Prudence.*] Who is your friend?

Prudence. The man of all Paris who loves you the most.

Camille. Indeed! Tell Nanine to place another knife and fork upon the supper table; for I dare say that love will never take away his appetite.

Prudence. Camille, I am serious. That young man loves you almost to madness.

Camille. Yes! But he will not go mad.

[*Olimpe presents Armand to Gaston.*]

Gaston. Duval! Oh, yes; I heard that name before. Are you any relation to Monsieur Duval, that gruff, crusty old gentleman, who was sometime Receiver-General at Tours?

Armand. Oh, yes! He is my father. Do you know him?

Gaston. I have had that pleasure. I met him at the house of the Baroness de Nersay. Also your mother, Madam Duval, who was a very beautiful and charming lady.

Armand. Alas, sir! she has been dead for three years.

Gaston. Pardon me, sir! I was not aware of it, or I should not have recalled her memory.

Armand. Oh, sir! you can never offend by reminding me

of my mother; for next to possessing affections so beautiful and pure as hers, is the remembrance of them when they are beyond our reach.

Gaston. You are an only child.

Armand. Oh, no! I have a dear sister. [*They go up.*]

Camille [*To Prudence.*] I begin to like your friend.

Prudence. I guessed it would be so; and so I told him before we came.

Camille. And did he really tell you he loves me?

Prudence. To be sure he did, and more; I knew it long ago. But you laugh so at the idea of love, that I did not dare to say so.

Olimpe. What are you two whispering about there?

Camille. Listen and you shall know. Monsieur de Varville, will you ever cease that noise?

Varville. Noise! Why you told me to play all the time.

Camille. That was when I was alone with you; but I need no pastime now.

Prudence. Well, as I was saying, for two years you have been his only thought. You may remember when you were ill a year ago, before you went to Bagneres, that during the three months you were confined to bed, you were told a young man called every day to learn how you were; but never left his name.

Camille. Oh, I remember.

Prudence. It was he.

Camille. Monsieur Duval.

Armand. Madam?

Camille. Do you know what they are telling me here:— that when I was ill a year ago, you called each day to learn how I was.

Armand. It is true, madam.

Camille Ah, Monsieur Varville, do you hear that?

Varville. Why I haven't known you a whole year.

Camille. And Monsieur Duval has known me just *five minutes.* [*Nanine and servants bring in supper table.*]

Prudence. That's right, Nanine, you're a sensible girl.

I certainly should have died with hunger if that table had not appeared.

Varville. Adieu, Camille, I am going.

Camille. I don't believe you.

Varville. You may, for I am off.

Camille. When shall I see you again?

Varville. Whenever you please.

Camille. Well, that is the most agreeable thing you have said to-night. Adieu! [EXIT VARVILLE.]

Olimpe. Adieu, Monsieur de Varville; don't forget your promise.

Gaston. Here, save your politeness; you will want it presently.

Camille. Now, my friends, to supper. Come, be seated. Armand you will sit next to me. [*They sit at table.*]

Prudence. Well, Camille, I think you treat that poor Count de Varville very badly.

Camille. Poor? You would not think him poor if you heard him counting over his revenue.

Olimpe. I wish he would count some of it over to me.

Gaston. Are you not satisfied, madam, with your present choice?

Olimpe. Well I ought to be, after that beautiful present you made me the other day. Camille, you cannot guess what he gave me on my birth day.

Camille. No, what was it?

Olimpe. A carriage.

Camille. A carriage! I am sure that was a very handsome present.

Olimpe. But I have no horses; and he wont buy me any.

Camille. Never mind—they will follow. Keep the carriage.

Olimpe. Alas! it is only a candy one.

Gaston. My dear girl, if you desire to prove the sincerity of your affections, love me for myself alone.

Olimpe. There's a modest request.

Prudence. What is that dish?

Gaston. Partridges.

Prudence. Give me some of them.

Gaston. A *wing* you mean.

Prudence. Monsieur Gaston, you are a boy.

Gaston. You must forgive me, I was not aware that ladies' appetites grew with their age.

Prudence. Age! And what age do you suppose I am!

Gaston. I do not know. Indeed I never studied ancient history. But you do not look more than forty, upon my honor.

Prudence. Forty! Thirty-six, if you please.

Gaston. Forty and thirty-six. Seventy—well, it does look more like that, I confess.

Prudence. Camille, will you speak to Monsieur Gaston? He is doing all he can to take away my appetite. And what are *you* doing there? You are not eating at all. Hand me some oysters, dear, and fill up Monsieur Duval's glass.

Camille. Good! Let us fill to my health, Armand!

Ail. To the health of Camille!

Camille. Gaston, you have not helped Olimpe.

Gaston. Haven't I, though?

Prudence. Come sit by me. I'll help you. Gaston has no idea of how to administer to a delicate appetite.

Gaston. Madam Prudence, have you ever had your throat examined!

Olimpe. Don't heed him, Madam Duverney. He is thinking of Amanda's throat, and the time she caught cold in the yellow carriage.

Camille. Oh, by the way, yes! What was that about the yellow carriage? Do let me hear it.

Gaston. My dear, will you come sit by me! I'll mix a salad for you.

Prudence. No, thank you, she is better here. Will you have another bird, my dear?

Gaston. That old woman must have a cast-iron stomach.

Prudence. What do you have supper for, if it is not to eat?

Olimpe. Why, you see Prudence, sometimes persons have suppers prepared for them that they do *not* eat; and sometimes persons go to great expense to have a supper served up in elegant style, a little out of town, and invite a beautiful girl to sup with them; and when they call to accompany her, they arrive just in time to see her drive off to the supper with another, and in the very yellow carriage they had brought for her!

Gaston. Mademoiselle Olimpe, that was a very stupid story!

Olimpe. But the sequel is very interesting. Shall I tell it?

All—(except Gaston.) Yes! yes! the sequel.

Camille. Let us drink to the hero of the yellow carriage.

All. To the hero of the yellow carriage!

Gaston. I'll drink, if it's only for the sake of the wine. Down goes the yellow carriage.

Camille. Now for a dance. Clear away the table.

Prudence. I have not finished yet.

Camille. A polka! A polka!

[*They dance. Camille grows sick.*]

Gaston. What's the matter, Camille?

Camille. Nothing! That cough again. That's all.

Armand. You are ill, madam!

Prudence. Give her something to eat.

Camille. A glass of water, please. I will be better soon. It is nothing. See, I am well already. Monsieur Duval, and you, Gaston, step into the other room, and before you have your segars lit, I will be with you. [*Aside to the ladies.*] Go with them. I am not well.

Prudence. Yes, let us leave her. She is better alone when these attacks arrive. [*Aside.*] It is always the way. Just as we are enjoying ourselves, on comes that cough again, and all our fun is over.

[Exeunt Gaston, Prudence and Olimpe.

Armand. [*Aside.*] Poor girl!

Camille. How pale I am! Ah!

Armand. Well, Mademoiselle, how do you feel now?

Camille. Ah, Monsieur Armand, is it you? Better, thank you. I have grown used to these of late.

Armand. You are killing yourself. I would I had the right to save you from yourself.

Camille. It is too late. Why, what's the matter with you?

Armand. You have made me ill.

Camille. Don't be foolish. Pray go into the next room, and enjoy yourself with the others. See, they do not heed me.

Armand. Ah, Camille, let me be your nurse—your doctor. I will guard you like a brother—shield you from this feverish existence, which is bringing you to your grave—surround you with a thousand little cares that will make you in love with life—then when you are strong and well, and can enjoy it, I will be as your guiding star, and lead your thoughts to find content in a home more worthy of you.

Camille. Monsieur Duval, if you would not offend me, let us change this subject. Do not deceive yourself—you cannot deceive me. You are not speaking to the cherished daughter of society ; but to a woman of the world—friendless, fearless—loved by those whose vanity she gratifies—despised by those who ought to pity her.

Armand. Camille, have you a heart?

Camille. Why do you ask?

Armand. Because, if you have, you could not make so light a matter of my words.

Camille. Are you really serious?

Armand. Very serious.

Camille. Prudence told me you were sentimental.

Armand. Prudence could not tell you how I love you.

Camille. And you still think you love me?

Armand. Camille, I cannot jest. This is the most serious moment of my life. My destiny is in your hands. You are young, lovely, loveable. The world in which you live is at your feet—smiles when you smile—is gay when you are gay. But does it weep with you, and in your sad and silent hours, does it hover around you with its care, and cheer you with its love? No! No! Then leave this tainted sphere. It is not worthy of you. Listen to the voice of one who truly loves you. Give me leave to find your heart, and teach it how to throb anew—to make it my shrine, my sanctuary, my home.

Camille. Are you sure you would take good care of it?

Armand. Trust me.

Camille. For how long?

Armand. Forever.

Camille. How long has this lasted?

Armand. For two years.

Camille. How came it you never told me of this before?

Armand. I never knew you until now.

Camille. You could very easily have made my acquaintance. When I was ill, and you came each day to inquire after me, why did you not ask to see me?

Armand. Pardon me!

Camille. Why, you loved me then?

Armand. Yes, too well to take a liberty I would not allow another to take in the house of the woman I respected.

Camille. So you really think you love me?

Armand. When you shall give me the right to say so, you will one day learn how well.

Camille. It were better never told.

Armand. And why?

Camille. Because it can result in but one of two things. First, that I will not believe it; or, believing it, cause you to wish I never had. I am but a sorrowful companion, at the best. Always sick, impatient, nervous, fretful—or, if gay, a gayety more terrible than tears—expensive, too—a revenue of thirty thousand francs, and always in debt. This may do for the dear old Duke, who loves me as his child, has plenty

2

of money, and no one to spend it. It would not do for you. Now we'll talk sense, Give me your hand. Let us join the others, and I'll light your segar.

Armand. Excuse me, Camille. Enter if you will; but allow me to remain.

Camille. What's the matter?

Armand. Pardon me. I am not well.

Camille. Shall I prescribe for you?

Armand. Speak.

Camille. Go home and go to bed. Dream all night of some dear girl, more worthy of your love than I. If indeed you love me, you have wronged yourself. You are too good to be deceived. You love too well to be unloved. But love *wisely.* Choose from a holier sphere than this the woman you would love. Then seal that love upon the altar. Take her to your bosom fresh with a parent's blessing; or, if she have none, let her merit that of heaven!

Armand. Camille, have you ever loved?

Camille. Never.

Armand. Thanks! Thanks! If you but knew how I have sought to learn what you have told me in that little word—how I have followed in your path—how I have cherished for six months a little button which fell from your glove——

Camille. I would not believe it. I have heard these tales before.

Armand. You are right. I know not what I say. I am a fool! Yes, laugh! I deserve it all. Good night.

Camille. Armand!

Armand. Did you call?

Camille. Let us not part in anger.

Armand. Anger! Oh, Camille, if you could read my heart!

Camille. Then let us make it up. Come and see me often. We will speak of this again.

Armand. Ah, still you laugh.

Camille. Speak, Armand; I am not laughing now.

Armand. Will you be loved?

Camille. For how long?

Armand. For eternity!

Camille. Alas! my life *may* yet be happy—it cannot be long—and short as it may be, it may outlive your promise.

Armand. Now, who is melancholy?

Camille. Not I. The weight that chained me to her throne's removed, and all around breathes ecstacy! But it grows late, and you must away.

Armand. When shall I see you again?

Camille. [*Giving him a Camelia.*] When this little flower is faded, bring it back to me again.

Armand. Ah, Camille, you have made me blessed.

Camille. It is a strange flower, Armand—pale, scentless, cold; but sensitive as purity itself. Cherish it, and its beauty will excel the loveliest flower that grows; but wound it with a single touch, you never can recall its bloom, or wipe away the stain. Take it, and remember me. Now go.

Armand. Adieu!   [EXIT.

Camille. He loves me. There is a new found meaning in those simple words that never fell upon my ears before.

[*Camille goes to piano and plays. Singing and revelry is heard in adjoining room.* PRUDENCE, OLIMPE, AND GASTON ENTER *dressed fantastically in each other's hats and bonnets.*]

Camille. What on earth have you been doing?

Prudence. We have been amusing ourselves in honor of the new alliance.

Gaston. Yes, I am to be bride.

Prudence. No! Bridesmaid, you mean.

Gaston. [*Mimicking a lady.*] If I can't be bride, I shan't be anything else, I assure you.

Olimpe. Now let's rehearse the bridal dance.

Gaston. Oh, yes! A dance! A dance! Camille, play for us!

[*Camille plays on Piano. Fantastic dance.*]

END OF ACT.

ACT SECOND.

SCENE:—*Same as in act first.*

NANINE AND PRUDENCE DISCOVERED—CAMILLE ENTERS AS
CURTAIN RISES.

Camille. Ah, Prudence, you are come. Have you seen the Duke?

Prudence. Yes, here is something he sent you. [*Gives a packet of bank notes.*] My dear Camille, can you lend me three or four hundred francs? I am in need of a little money this morning.

Camille. Here they are. [*Gives Money.*] Did you tell the Duke of my intention to go to the country?

Prudence. Yes.

Camille. What did he say?

Prudence. That you are right—that nothing could be better for your health. And you will go?

Camille. I hope so. I was to see that house to-day again.

Prudence. What is the rent of it?

Camille. Two thousand francs.

Prudence. Camille, this looks very much like love.

Camille. I am afraid it is. It certainly is *something*. Listen how my heart beats.

Prudence. Oh, dear! this is an awful state of affairs. I wonder if it's *catching?*

Camille. It is near ten o'clock. He will soon be here. [*Door-bell rings.*] Ah, 'tis he! Run, Nanine, open the door.

[EXIT NANINE.

Prudence. You are mistaken. No one rang.

Camille. Even so. There is a speechless thrilling in my breast that tells me he is near.

Prudence. I am off.

Camille. Stay till he comes.

Prudence. Oh, no! I must go home and pray for you. You are in danger.

Camille. Perhaps I am.

ARMAND ENTERS.

Armand. Camille!

Camille. Armand! I knew your ring.

Prudence. Oh, you ungrateful man!

Armand. Forgive me, Prudence. I saw but *her!* Are you well?

Prudence. Yes, all are well now; so I will leave you, my children. An old woman is like a doctor,—never thought of when all goes well; but the first we send for when there's a wound to heal.   [EXIT PRUDENCE.

Camille. Come sit by me.

Armand. Here I am.

Camille. Do you love me more and more?

Armand. No!

Camille. How?

Armand. I love you so much, I have no room for more.

Camille, What have you been doing to-day?

Armand. I was to see Prudence, Nichette, Gustave— everywhere that I could hear your name.

Camille. You have been idle.

Armand. No, I wrote to my father, telling him he need no longer await me at Tours.

Camille. You may offend him. That must not be.

Armand. No, he will not expect me. What have *you* been doing all day?

Camille. Thinking of you.

Armand. True?

Camille. True! And manufacturing grand projects.

Armand. What were they?

Camille. I must not tell.

Armand. I have no secrets from you.

Camille. Listen. I cannot tell you at present what my

projects are; but should they succeed, I can tell you their result.

Armand. What will it be?

Camille. To bring me nearer you.

Armand. Oh, tell me how.

Camille. By passing the summer months together in some quiet spot in the country. In a few days from this I shall know the *result*, and you shall know the *cause*. Till then you must not ask me.

Armand. And is it you alone, Camille, who have formed these projects?

Camille. What a strange question

Armand. Answer me.

Camille. Well, 'tis I alone.

Armand. And you alone will execute them?

Camille. I, alone.

Armand. Camille, have you ever read Manon Lescaut?

Camille. I have.

Armand. Do you remember the story of Manon?

Camille. It has been some time since I read the book.

Armand. I will remind you. She loved a young man, who loved her as his wife; but who was poor—too poor to meet the large expense her taste and style demanded. She, too, formed a project, and named it to a wealthy friend, who gladly aided it—gave her all she asked—and while she thanked him for the wealth he had bestowed upon her, she smiled upon *another*, upon whom she lavished it. Camille, you are too truthful to be that woman; and I am too honorable to be that man.

Camille. What does this mean?

Armand. That if your schemes at all resemble hers, I will not be a partner in them.

Camille. Good. Let us change the theme. It has been a beautiful day.

Armand. [*Looking out of window.*] Beautiful!

Camille. The Champs Elysees crowded?

Armand. Crowded!

Camille. Change of the moon to-night, I believe?

Armand. Devil take the moon. Camille, I am not thinking of the moon.

Camille. Neither am I.

Armand. What would you have me do? You know that I am jealous of your very thoughts, and what you told me a moment ago——

Camille. Are you going to be a second edition of that book? Listen to me. I *love you.* I never told you so before. For that love I ask your confidence. You are not jealous of that poor old man the Duke. You know the sacred sentiments which bind him to my interests. That I am not where he would place me, was the fault of those who drove me from it. It was no act of his. Could he see where he would have me, his aged heart would know another joy. Let me have my way. It shall lead me to your love, be sure! Is it all right?

Armand. But—but—

Camille. Come—come! Say it is.

Armand. No, not yet.

Camille. Then good night.

Armand. Good night! Why you would not send me away so soon?

Camille. No—no; but—you may remain a little longer.

Armand. Perhaps you are expecting some one?

Camille. Are you going to commence again?

Armand. You will not deceive me now.

Camille. How long have I known you?

Armand. Four days.

Camille. If I did not love you, I would not know you one. So if you love me, say good night, and don't complain.

Armand. Oh, forgive me.

Camille. If this continues, I shall spend my life in forgiving you.

Armand. No—no! It is my last offence. Good night.

Camille. Come early to-morrow, and we will breakfast together.

Armand. Once more, good night! [Exit.

Camille. Life! Life! You are a puzzle! Who would have made me believe four days ago, that that man, a stranger to me, would to-day so occupy my heart and thought? Can this be love; or is it madness? Does he indeed love me? Can he forget what I *have been* and what I *am*. *Ah, that past—this present—if I could tear it from my heart!* Armand, why—why have you come across my path? I was happy till you came; and now—oh! I dare not think of what I am! Yet in this struggle between hope and fear, there's something whispers me of happier hours. *I love, and I am loved!* Ah, there is wealth enough of joy in those dear words to cancel an eternity of care!

[NANINE ENTERS, *announces* " *Monsieur le Count de Varville,*" *and* EXITS. ENTER VARVILLE.]

Camille. Good evening, Count.

Varville. Good evening, Camille. You are looking charming! Are you well?

Camille. Very.

Varville. You got my note?

Camille. I did.

Varville. Just half-past ten o'clock. [*Looking at his watch.*] You see I am punctual.

Camille. You wrote me that you wished to speak with me on business.

Varville. Yes. Have you been to supper?

Camille. Why do you ask?

Varville. Because, if you will come and sup with me, we can talk this matter over in quiet.

Camille. Are you very hungry?

Varville. Yes, I am. That dinner at the club has quite given me an appetite.

Camille. What are they doing at the club to-night?

Varville. Playing when I left.

Camille. Who won?

Varville. Monsieur Gaston, whom I met here the other night. Apropos, who was that odd-looking sort of person—Monsieur—Monsieur something, that Prudence introduced?

Camille. That *gentleman* was Monsieur Armand Duval, my friend.

Varville. Apropos, did any one leave here as I entered?

Camille. Not that I know of. Who was it?

Varville. That is precisely what I should like to know. As I ascended from the carriage, some one watched me until I reached the door, and when he saw my face, he hurried away as if I had been a creditor.

Camille. Well, Count, let's to business. What have you got to say to me?

Varville. Camille, who are your creditors?

Camille. I have not the remotest idea.

Varville. Why, you told me that you were twenty thousand francs in debt. Is it paid?

Camille. Not that I know of.

Varville. But you know the parties to whom you owe it?

Camille. I have not that honor, personally. I know their address.

Varville. Where is it?

Camille. Somewhere there. [*Hands an account book.*]

Varville. Yes, here it is all summed up. Twenty—why here are ten more. It is thirty thousand francs.

Camille. Why so it is! I had forgotten. Count, have I not kept those accounts in very fine order?

Varville. Yes, they appear to be in a remarkable state of preservation.

Camille. They will look better when receipted.

Varville. And is it necessary that they should be paid?

Camille. Absolutely.

Varville. Camille, suppose you charge me with this little affair! I am very idle, and want something to do.

Camille. Oh, Monsieur de Varville, it may occupy your time too much. But since you will have it so, the exercise may do you good.

Varville. Will you have the receipt now?

Camille. No—no; you may bring it in a week or so.

Varville, [*Aside.*] A week or so! Varville, you have been a fool!

[ENTER NANINE.]

Nanine. Madam, a man brought this letter, and said that it must reach you immediately.

Camille. Who can write to me at this hour? [*Looks at the letter.*] Armand! What can this mean? [*Reads.* "Madam, I cannot be trifled with even by the woman whom I love. At the very moment that I quitted your house, the Count de Varville entered it. I am neither a Count nor a millionaire. Forgive me, if in my poverty I have been too bold. Let us forget that we ever met, or that we ever thought we loved. When you receive this letter, I shall have quitted Paris. Armand."

Nanine. Is there any answer, madam?

Camille. None! It is well. [EXIT NANINE.] Another dream dispelled. I have deserved it. I should have known better! What had I to do with love? Oh, I am sick.

Varville. What was in that letter, Camille?

Camille. Good news for you, Count. You have gained thirty thousand francs.

Varville. It is the first letter of the kind that ever came in my way! But how?

Camille. You need not attend to that little affair for me. I like to be in debt. It occupies my mind.

Varville. Have your creditors died?

Camille. Worse than that! I was in love.

Varville. You?

Camille. I!

Varville. With whom?

Camille. One who did not love me, as often happens! A man who is poor, as often happens! [*Gives him the letter.*] Read!

Varville. [*Aside.*] Phew! I understand now why those debts no longer trouble you. [*Aloud.*] My dear Camille, this is indeed too bad, and from a *friend,* too! So Monsieur Duval, it appears, is very jealous.

Camille. You have invited me to supper?

Varville. I have. We are waited for.

Camille. Come, I want air.

Varville. [*Aside.*] This begins to look serious. [*Aloud.*] Camille, you are agitated. What is the matter?

Camille. Nothing. Nanine! Nanine! my shawl and bonnet! Quick!

[ENTER NANINE.]

Nanine. Which, Madam?

Camille. Any one at all. A light shawl will answer.

[EXIT NANINE.

Varville. You will be cold.

Camille. Cold! I am on fire!

ENTER NANINE, *with shawl and bonnet.*

Nanine. Shall I sit up for you, Madam?

Camille. No, retire. I will not return until late. Come, Count, come! [EXEUNT CAMILLE AND VARVILLE.

Nanine. There is something very strange going on here. Camille is very much excited. It was that letter, I know, that did it all. Ah, here it is! [*Takes up the letter from table and reads.*] So, so,—Monsieur Duval—that is how you do. Going to quit Paris! That is a very good sign, I never knew a lover of Camille who vowed he was going to leave Paris on her account that did not keep me answering the bell for three months after. [ENTER PRUDENCE.] Ah, good evening, Madame Duverney.

Prudence. Where is Camille?

Nanine. She has just gone out to sup with the Count de Varville.

Prudence. She received a letter a few minutes since?

Nanine. She did: It was from Monsieur Duval.

Prudence. What did he say?

Nanine. Nothing.

Prudence. When will she return?

Nanine. I do not know. She said I might retire—that she would not return early. I thought you had retired long ago.

Prudence. So I had, and fast asleep, when I was awakened by a pulling of the bell, which is sounding in my ears ever since. So Camille is gone out, is she? I thought that letter would make mischief.

Camille. [*Entering quickly.*] Give me my mantle, Nanine; this shawl's too light. [EXIT NANINE. *To Prudence.*] Oh, how you frightened me! What's the matter?

Prudence. That is just what I want to know. [*Points to window.*] Armand is there.

Camille. Well, what is that to me?

Prudence. He wishes to see you.

ENTER NANINE, *with mantle, which she places on* CAMILLE'S *shoulders.*

Camille. What for? I do not wish to see him. Good-night. The Count is waiting for me.

Prudence. Stay, Camille, you had better see him. He is very unhappy; and better that you should explain this matter to him than that he should demand an explanation from the Count.

Camille. He has changed his mind, then! I thought he had quitted Paris?

Prudence. Camille, have you forgotten that he loves you?

Camille. Give me my mantle, Nanine, I must go.

Nanine. You have it, Madam.

Camille. That man has almost killed me.

Prudence. Then perhaps you had better not see him again. Let him go, and let matters rest where they are.

Camille. [*Weeping.*] That is your advice?

Prudence. It is.

Camille. What else did he say?

Prudeuce. That he will tell you himself. I see how it is. Love—this love—the more you fan it, the more it burns. [*Calls at window.*] Armand! [*To Camille.*] But the Count?

Camille. He will wait.

Prudence. Had you not better send him away at once?

Camille. You are right. Nanine, go tell Mon. de Var-ville that I am not well—that I cannot go out to-night—that he must excuse me,

Nanine. Yes, Madam. [Exit.

Camille. I feel better now.

Prudence. [*At window.*] Armand, come! He will not require a second invitation, I dare say.

Camille. You will stay here until he comes.

Prudence. No, I thank you. I will go and finish my dreams, and leave you to begin yours again. Oh, dear! It seems as if the world was on fire, and all the bells were ring-ing in my head. [Exit.

Nanine. [Entering.] The Count has gone, Madam.

Camille. What did he say?

Nanine. Nothing; but he appeared very much annoyed. [Exit.

[Enter Armand.]

Armand. Ah, Camille, can you forgive me?

Camille. Do you deserve it? Why did you write me that cruel letter? You have made me ill.

Armand. What would you have me do? I saw the Count de Varville enter here the very moment you had *hurried* me away. I knew not what I did. I could scarce believe my eyes. I wrote that letter—sent it. Forgive me, then, and remember, Camille, though I have known you only a few days, I have loved you two years.

Camille. Armand, from the first hour I met you, I have nourished the thought of passing the summer with you, far from Paris—far from the world. I said to myself, at the end of three months of his companionship and care, I will be re-stored to health and peace of mind. I will try to win his friendship—be worthy his esteem—and, on our return to Paris, instead of the hollow hearts and serpent tongues that crowd around me now, Armand shall be my only friend, pro-tector, brother! And so I dreamed, and dreamed, until that letter woke me. We must part. My position forbids me seeing you again, and every thing forbids me loving you.

Armand. Camille, you never loved me, or the Count had not been here to-night.

Camille. Another reason why you should not *love me.* You have position, friends, honor,—*be wise.* I have neither. I am young, gay, reckless, desperate—my name the sport of every tongue in Paris. If you *will* know me, take what is good of me, and leave the rest.

Armand. It was not thus you talked an hour ago.

Camille. True! I have reflected since.

Armand. Camille, I love you. The feeling that I entertain for you has become a part of me. My destiny hung upon your love. Thinking I had won it, I soared upon my hopes beyond my height, and it is in falling from them that I am crushed. Since it is so, let us part. Farewell! You do not love me.

Camille. Oh, you know not what you say. Stay! I would speak to you; but dare not.

Armand. Speak, Camille, I listen.

Camille. Armand, every heart has its silent hours, and so has mine; and in those hours, I often sit and think there is a happier life than the one I lead, if I could but find it. And there are moments when visions of a future flit across my brain. I think if I can lend a charm to such a life as this, and win the admiration and respect of the worthless crowd who follow me, what would it be in the sacred circle of a home, among those who loved and cherished me? Can such a future be in store for me, I ask. And then the past spreads o'er me, like a pall. A merry laugh bursts forth in mockery, and I am gay again.

Armand. Go on.

Camille. Day follows day,—and so I live. I have admirers—lovers, if you will—the first in their vanity, the last in their esteem. Friends, too, like Prudence. And so the tide of time glides on, one stream of vanity, shame, and lies. *You* came, and with you many an untold hope. I heard your voice—I saw your tears—and built my faith upon your love.

Then I dreamed of innocence—of purity. Your letter came next, and with it came reproach. Two years ago I last heard reproach. A poor, friendless, sickly girl, disgusted with that world where she had sold her smiles for gold, had dared to enter the abode of peace—the charmed circle of society. Whatever her history had been, long-suffering had purified her thoughts—her heart was pure—*she sinned no more.* But society was outraged. With iron hand it flung her from its shore, and left her, beaconless, upon the sea where she is wrecked !

Armand. These words are not for me.

Camille. No ; but *these* words are for me. *Points to letter.*] They warn me of another blast. I know my safety, and will not peril it. Why should I, and for what? For jeers, contempt, and scorn ? No, no, no—I have tried that. That is your way, this is mine.

[ENTER NANINE, *quickly with a letter.*]

Nanine. A letter, Madam.

Camille. Who sent it ?

Nanine. The Count de Varville.

Armand. [*Suddenly.*] The Count de Varville ! Now, Camille, this is the touchstone of your worth ! My *life*—your *honor*, hang upon your answer !

[*Camille tears letter, and throws it toward Nanine.*]

Camille. Give him that!

[*Throws herself on Armand's breast.*]

END OF ACT.

ACT THIRD.

SCENE :—*A room in a Country House.*
NANINE DISCOVERED.

Prudence. [ENTERING.] Where is Camille?

Nanine. She is in the garden, with Mademoiselle Nichette and Monsieur Gustave. Monsieur Armand has gone to Paris, and they have come to spend the day with Madam. [EXIT.

Prudence. I will join them.

Camille. [ENTERING.] Ah, Prudence, you are come. Is all arranged?

Prudence. Yes; or soon will be, I hope.

Camille. Where are the papers?

Prudence. Here they are. The man will be here to-day to see if they are right. So I will go to dinner, for I am dying of hunger.

ENTER NICHETTE AND GUSTAVE.

Camille. Come, sit down. Tell me: how do you like the way we live here?

Nichette. Oh, I think you must be very happy!

Camille. You are right—I am.

Nichette. And *you* are right, Camille, when you say that happiness is in the heart. How often have I said to Gustave, I wish Camille would meet with some one who would love and cherish her—who would win her from the feverish life she leads, and teach her contentment in one more tranquil and enduring.

Camille. Well, you have your wish. I love—and I am happy.

Nichette. Oh, it is so sweet to be happy! And we are all happy,— are we not, Gustave?

Gustave. I believe we are. If, before to-day, Nichette and I have had a separate wish, it was, Camille, to see you where you are.

Camille. Thanks, Gustave.

Nichette. After all, happiness does not cost much, if one can only find the right material. If you could but see where I live—two little chambers in the fifth story, in La Rue Blanche—a window that overlooks half of Paris—a trellis, where I have planted a geranium, the first flower Gustave ever gave me—and how it grows!—no wonder, for I sit and sew by it, and watch it all day. Oh, you should see my little home. It is so cozy—just large enough to hold content.

Gustave. It must like going up-stairs better than I do.

Nichette. Camille, do you hear that saucy fellow? You cannot guess what he wants me to do—to quit embroidering, and not work any more. He will buy me a carriage next.

Gustave. That will come. Then, Camille, you will drive out with us,—will you not?

Camille. Yes, Gustave, that I will.

Nichette. Oh, we will have such a time! You must know that Gustave has a rich old uncle, who is going to make him his heir. But I forgot to tell you—Gustave is a lawyer now, if you please!

Camille. Indeed,—you shall plead my first case.

Nichette. Oh, he has pleaded already!

Camille. Did he gain?

Gustave. No. My client was condemned to ten years' hard labor.

Nichette. Yes! I was there,—and I was so glad!

Camille. Glad! Why so?

Nichette. Because the man deserved it. I don't believe in those great men who fold their arms and say: "Gentlemen, I have had, in my time, the case of a man who had killed a father, a mother, and her children! Well, sirs, I worked at that case night and day, until I gained it. He was acquitted. But I confess it cost me a great deal of labor—and in

3

all modesty, I say, that nothing short of the most sublime talents could have restored that ornament to the society which he had adorned."

Camille. And now that he is a lawyer, Nichette will soon be a bride. Is it not so?

Nichette. If he behaves himself.

Gustave. You hear the conditions. Then, Camille, may we not hope that you, too, may be a bride some day?

Camille. The bride of whom?

Gustave. Of Armand.

Camille. Armand! That can never be! Armand would marry me to-morrow if I would have it so; but I love him too well to merit his reproach.

Gustave. Camille, you are so generous.

Camille. Not generous, Gustave, but *just.* The woman does not love the man she would degrade. There are impressions made in life which time may erase from the memory, but never from the heart. My past is *there.* A sea of tears could not wash one pang away, which tells me I am unworthy to be Armand Duval's wife. But let us talk of something else. I have so much happiness, why ask for more? To be near the man I love—to hear his voice—to know his truth! —Oh my dream of life has grown so blissful, peaceful, calm, I would not dare to wake it by wearying heaven with a wish beyond the present.

Nichette. How do you pass the time, Camille?

Camille. I really cannot tell—it flies so fast. After taking a long walk, with Armand, I read to him or he reads to me. Then I feed my birds, and listen to them sing. I often sit by him and sew, while he talks to me of the future, until I think I I am in another world. And then, as you have just seen, in this simple dress, with my great straw hat, I skip along the fields, or sail upon the water by his side, I feel I am a child again! And when sad thoughts steal by me, as they often do, I wrap myself up in Armand's love, and all is bright again!

Gustave. I begin to think Nichette does not love me.

Camille. Because—

Gustave. Because she does not talk of me as you do of Armand.

Camille. She has no need. You are hers—the jewel of her life—while mine is only *lent.* I may admire but dare not hope to own it. But let that pass. Are not these sweet flowers which Armand gave me this morning? I used to spend as much in boquets as would have kept a poor family a whole year; and now, these simple sprays culled by his hand, seem to load the air with perfume. Oh, how happy I am. But you do not know all.

Nichette. What can it be?

Gustave. Who says Nichette is curious?

Camille. You said awhile ago that I should see *your* home. Perhaps I will see it soon. Unknown to Armand, I am going to sell my house in Paris, pay all my debts—rent an apartment near yours—furnish it precisely the same—and we will live together forgetting and forgotten. In the summer we will live in the country, hire a little cottage—do all our own work—live alone—and who will be happier than we?

Nichette. How strange that is. That is just what Gustave and I were wishing to-day that you would do.

Nanine. [ENTERING.] Madam, there is a gentleman in the hall who wishes to see to you.

Camille. You see I did not jest. That is the man who has charge of the sale. So walk into the garden, you and Gustave. He will soon be gone, and I will join you. [EXIT. GUSTAVE *and* NICHETTE.] Bid him enter.

EXIT NANINE. ENTER DUVAL.

Duval. Mademoiselle Camille Gauthier?

Camille. It is I, Monsieur. To whom have I the honor of speaking?

Duval. To Monsieur Duval.

Camille. To Monsieur Duval?

Duval. Yes, Mademoiselle, the father of Armand.

Camille. Monsieur Armand is not here, sir.

Duval. I know it. But it is with you that I would speak, and I wish you to listen. You are not only compromising but ruining my son.

Camille. You are deceived, sir. I am here beyond the reach of scandal; and I accept nothing from your son.

Duval. Which means that he has fallen so low as to be a sharer of the gain which you accept from others.

Camille. Pardon me, sir. I am a woman, and in my own house,—two reasons that should plead in my behalf to your more generous courtesy. The tone in which you addressed me is not what I have been accustomed to, and more than I can listen to from a gentleman whom I have the honor to see for the first time. I pray you will allow me to retire.

Duval. Stay, Madam, when one finds himself face to face with you, it is hard to think those things are so. Oh, I was told that you were a dangerous woman.

Camille. Yes, sir! dangerous to myself.

Duval. It is not less true, however, that you are ruining my son.

Camille. Sir, I repeat, with all the respect I have for Armand's father, that you are wrong.

Duval. Then what is the meaning of this letter to my lawyer, which apprises me of Armand's intention to dispose of his property, the gift of a dying mother? [*Gives her a letter.*]

Camille. I assure you, sir, that if this is Armand's act, he has done so without my knowledge; for he knew well that had he offered such a gift, I would refuse it.

Duval. Indeed, you have not always spoken thus!

Camille. True, sir; but I have not always loved.

Duval. And now—

Camille. I am now no longer what I was.

Duval. These are very fine words.

Camille. What can I say to convince you? I swear by the love I bear your son, the holiest thing that ever filled my heart, that I was ignorant of the transaction.

Duval. Still you must live by some means?

Camille. You force me, sir, to be explicit. So far from resembling other associations of my life, this has made me penniless. I pray you read that paper. [*Handing a paper.*] It contains a list of all that I possess on earth. When you were announced just now, I thought you were the person to whom I had sold them.

Duval. A bill of sale of all your furniture, pictures, plate, &c., with which to pay your creditors—the surplus to be returned to you. Have I been deceived?

Camille. You have, sir. I know that my life has been clouded—my name as a forbidden word. I have not forgotten that. Oh, no, no! It is traced upon my heart in colors that can never fade. The love I bear your son but magnifies their form, which I would give the last drop of my blood to cancel or efface. Oh, you do not know me, sir? You can never know how purely I do love your son, and how he loves me! It is his love which has saved me from myself and made me what I am. I have been so happy for three months! And you, sir, are his father. You are good, I am sure. I know you would not harm me. Then let me entreat you will not tell him ill of me, or he will believe you, for he loves you so; and I also love and honor you, because you are *his father!*

Duval. Pardon me for the manner in which I presented myself to you. I was angry at my son for his ingratitude to his dead mother, in disposing of her gift to him. I pray you, pardon.

Camille. Oh, sir, it is you who have all to pardon. I can only bless you for those kind words. I pray you take a chair.

Duval. It is in the name of these sentiments, which, you say, are so sacred to you, that I am about to ask of you a sacrifice greater than any you have yet performed.

Camille. Oh, heaven!

Duval. Listen, my child, and patiently, to what I have to say.

Camille. Oh, sir, I pray you let us speak no more. I know you are going to ask me something terrible. I have been expecting this. I was too happy. Yet over my brightest hour there has always hung a cloud. It was the shadow of your frown.

Duval. Camille, I am not going to chide, but *supplicate.* You love my son—so do I. We are both desirous of his happiness—jealous of those who could contribute to it more than we. I speak to you as a father, and ask of you the happiness of both my children.

Camille. Of both your children?

Duval. Yes, Camille, of both. I have a daughter, young, beautiful, and pure as an angel. She loves as you do. That love has been the dream of her life. But the family of the man about to marry her, has learned the relation between you and Armand, and declared the withdrawal of their consent unless he gives you up. You see, then, how much depends on you. Let me entreat you in the name of your love for her brother, to save my daughter's peace.

Camille. You are very good, sir, to deign to speak such words as these. I understand you, and you are right. I will at once quit Paris, and remain away from Armand for sometime. It will be a sacrifice, I confess; but I will make it for *your* sake. Besides his joy at my return will make amends for my absence. You will allow him to write me after your daughter is married?

Duval. Thanks, my child; but I fear you do not wholly understand me. I would ask more.

Camille. What could I do more?

Duval. A temporary absence will not suffice.

Camille. Ah, you would not have me quit Armand forever?

Duval. You must.

Camille. Never! To separate us now would be more than cruel—it would be a crime. Oh, sir! you have never loved! You know not what it is to be left without a home, a friend, a father, or a family. When Armand forgave my faults he swore to be all these. I have grafted life and hope on him till they and he are one. Oh do not tear him from me the little while I have to live! I am not well, sir! I have been ill for months. A sudden shock would kill me. Ask any thing but this. Oh, do not drive me to despair! See, I am at your feet!

Duval. Rise, Camille! I know that I demand a great sacrifice from your heart; but one that, for your own good, you are fatally forced to yield. Listen. You have known Armand three months, and you love him. Are you sure you have not deceived yourself, and that even now you do not begin to tire of your new choice, and long for other conquests?

Camille. Oh, spare me, sir! Unworthy as the offering of my love may seem, Armand's heart was the first shrine in which it ever sought a sanctuary, and there it shall remain forever!

Duval. You think so now, perhaps; but sooner or later the truth must come. Youth is prodigal—old age exacting. Do you listen?

Camille. Do I listen? Oh, heaven!

Duval. You are willing to sacrifice every thing for my son; but should he accept this, what sacrifice could he make you in return? Say that Armand Duval is an honest man, and would marry you,—what kind of union would that be which has neither purity nor religion to recommend it to the grace of heaven, the smile of friends, or the esteem of the world? And what will be your fate to see the man who sacrificed position, honor, all for you, bowed down with shame of her who ought to be his pride?

Camille. Oh, my punishment is come!

Duval. Avoid what yet may come. Say that you love, both, as none have ever loved. The warmest sun will set at eve. And when the evening of your life steals on, Armand will seek elsewhere the charms he can no longer find in you; and with every trace of age upon *your* brow, a blush will rise on *his*, accusing him of youth, and hopes, and honor, lost for you!

Camille. My dream is past!

Duval. Dream no more, Camille; but wake to duty to yourself and to the man you love.

Camille.   Why—why do I live?

Duval.   And should you die, would you have your husband stand upon your grave, ashamed to breathe the name of her who lies there?   No, Camille, you are too proud for that.   I leave to your heart, to your reason, to your affection for my son, the sacrifice I might demand.   You will be proud some day of having saved Armand from a fate he would have regretted all his life—which would have brought on him the idle jest and scorn of every honorable man.   Pardon me, Camille; but you know the world too well to doubt the truth of what I say.   It is a father who implores you to save his child.   Come, *prove* to me you love my son.   Give me your hand.   Courage, Camille, courage!   [*She slowly gives her hand.*]   Bless you, bless you!   You have done your duty.

Camille.   Oh, I was fallen—fallen!   Why did I seek to rise?   Was it not ever thus?   When I have dared to soar beyond the meshes of corruption, vice and shame, some iron hand has dashed me back and chained me to the shore of infamy!   Oh, fool, fool, fool!   What have you to do with thoughts like these?   What man would call you wife?   What child would call you mother?   What virtuous home would set its door ajar to welcome in a pestilence?   But it is well—well—it brings me nearer to the close.   You speak, sir, of your daughter.   She is young, lovely, pure.   I once was all of these.   She loves and she is loved—honored and esteemed. These I may never be.   Still I would have the little that was good of me dwell in her chaste memory when I may be no more.   You desire, sir, that I separate from your son for his good, his honor and his fortune.   What am I to do?   Speak —I am ready!

Duval.   You must tell him that you do not love him.

Camille.   He will not believe me.

Duval.   You must leave Paris.

Camille.   He will follow me.

Duval.   What *will* you do?

Camille.   I must teach him to despise me.

Duval. But, Camille, I fear—

Camille. Ah, fear nothing! He will hate me! I will teach him. I know how; for I have taught myself.

Duval. Armand must not know of this.

Camille. Sir, you do not know me yet; for I swear by the love I bear your son, that he shall never know from my lips what has transpired between us.

Duval. You are a noble girl! Is there aught that I can do for you?

Camille. When the heart that now is breaking lies pulseless in the grave—when the world records my very virtues to my blame—when Armand's voice shall rise with curses on my memory—tell him—Oh! tell him how I loved him! And now, I pray you will withdraw into that room. He may return each moment and discover our purpose. [EXIT DUVAL. *She goes to table to write.*] Oh, I cannot! Every word I trace seems to tear from my heart a hope that never can take root again. What shall I say? [*Reads what she has written.*] " Armand, in a few hours from this, the little flowers you gave me this morning will be withered on my breast, and in their place, Camelias, the badge of that life in which alone I can find happiness." Oh! heaven, forgive the injuries these words may bring to him, and the injustice they do my heart!

ENTER ARMAND.

Armand. Ah, Camille, here I am! What are you doing there?

Camille. Armand! Nothing!

Armand. You were writing as I entered.

Camille. No! That is—yes!

Armand. What does this mean? You are pale! To whom were you writing? Camille, let me see that letter.

Camille. I cannot.

Armand. I thought we had done with mystery.

Camille. And with suspicion.

Armand. Pardon me, Camille,—I was wrong. I entered

excited, and saw in you my own embarrassment. My father is arrived.

Camille. Have you seen him?

Armand. No; but he left at my house a letter, in which he reproaches me very bitterly. He has learned that I am here, and doubtless will pay me a visit this evening. Some idle tongues have been busy in informing him of our retreat. But let him come. I wish him to see you—to talk with you. He will be sure to love you. Or should he remain stern for awhile, and refuse his smiles, what of it? He can withhold his patronage from me; but he cannot separate me from your love. I will work, toil, labor for you, and think it a privilege and a joy, if I have but your smile to repay me at its close.

Camille. How he loves me! But you must be wise and not anger your father unnecessarily; for you know he has much cause to blame. He is coming, you say. Then I will retire awhile until he speaks with you—then I will return, and be with you again. I will fall at his feet, and implore him not to part us.

Armand. Camille, there is something passing in your mind that you would hide from me. It is not my words that agitate you so. You can scarcely stand. There is something wrong here. It is this letter. [*Snatches the letter from her.*]

Camille. Armand—that letter must not be read.

Armand. What does it contain?

Camille. A proof of my love for you. In the name of that love, return it to me unread, and ask to know no more.

Armand. Take it, Camille. I know it all. Prudence told me this morning, and it was that which took me to Paris. I know the sacrifice you would make, and while you were considering my happiness, I was not unmindful of yours. I have arranged it all unknown to you. Ah, Camille, how can I ever return such devotion, truth and love?

Camille. Well, now that you are satisfied, and know all, let us part —

Armand. Part?

Camille. I mean, let me retire. Your father will be here, you remember, and I would rather he would see you alone. I will be in the garden with Nichette and Gustave. You can call me when you want me. Oh, how—how can I ever part from you? You will calm your father, if he be irritated, and win him to forgive you. Will you not? Then we will be so happy—happy as we have always been since first we met! And you are happy,—are you not?—And have nothing to reproach me for,—have you? Since first I met you I welcomed in my heart of hearts your love, believing it a sign from heaven that the past had been forgiven. If I have ever caused your heart a pang, you will forgive me,—will you not? And when you recall, one day, the little proofs of love I have bestowed on you, you will not despise or curse my memory! Oh, do not—do not curse me, when you learn how I have loved you!

Armand. Camille, what does this mean?

Camille. Love for you!

Armand. But why these tears?

Camille. Oh, let them fall! I had forgotten. Do not heed them. I am such a silly girl! You know I often love to weep. See, I am calm now. They are all gone. Come, chase them away. [*He kisses her brow.*] See, now, they are all gone. No more tears but smiles. You, too, are smiling. Ah! I will live on that smile until we meet again? See, I too, can smile! You can read until your father comes, and think of me; for I shall never cease to think of you. Adieu, [*Aside.*] forever! [EXIT.

Armand. How she loves me. She fears my father may separate us. It is too late. The world would be a blank without her. [*Calls.*] Nanine! [ENTER NANINE.] A gentleman, my father, will arrive here presently. If he ask to see Madam, say that I am here awaiting him.

Nanine. I will, sir.

Armand. Give me a light. [*She gives a light and exits.*] Let me see what we have here. [*Takes letters from his pock-*

et.] I met Olimpe to-day. Always the same—busy with balls and fetes and revelries of all kinds. Poor fool! She has but one thought herself. Her heart is empty, and she tries to fill the void with noisy bustle and excitement. Here is an invitation to her ball next week—as if Camille could ever again lend her presence to such scenes. Seven o'clock! My father should be here. What book is this? I cannot read. It seems as if the time stood still when that girl is from my side. I will call her in. [*Rings bell.* NANINE ENTERS.] That gentleman will not be here to-night. Tell Madam to come in! It grows too cold to remain in the night air.

Nanine. Madam is not here, sir.

Armand. How? Where is she, then?

Nanine. I saw her go down the road. She told me to say to you, sir, that she would return presently.

Armand. Very well! [EXIT NANINE.] Where can she be gone? I think I see her form in the garden. [*Calls.*] Camille! Camille! No, there is no one there. [*Calls again.*] Nanine! Nanine! [*Rings bell impatiently.*] Nanine, I say! No answer! What can this mean? This silence makes me shudder! There is a desolation in that quiet that forebodes no good. Why did I suffer Camille to leave me? There was something she would hide from me. She appeared confused when I entered,—and then she wept! I will go —

As he hastens towards the door a MESSENGER ENTERS.

Messenger. Your pardon, sir. You are Monsieur Armand Duval?

Armand. I am.

Messenger. Here is a letter for you, sir?

Armand. Who gave it to you?

Messenger. A lady. The garden gate was open. There was no one about. I saw a light here, and I thought I might enter.

Armand. You were right. Leave me. [EXIT MESSENGER.] It is *her* handwriting. Why have I not the power to open it? I tremble like a child. [DUVAL ENTERS *unperceived and gazes*

intently upon Armand, who opens letter and reads aloud.]
" An hour after you will have received this letter, Armand, I
shall be with the Count de Varville." [*He staggers back, sees
his father, and falls on his breast.*] Father! my heart is
shattered!!

END OF ACT.

ACT FOURTH.

SCENE.—*A room in the house of Olimpe.*

*Parties dancing as curtain rises. Others at tables playing
cards.*

PRUDENCE, OLIMPE, GASTON AND GUSTAVE DISCOVERED.
At the close of the dance ARMAND ENTERS.]

Prudence. Why, here is Armand! We were just speaking of you a moment since.

Armand. And what were you saying?

Prudence. I was saying that you were at Tours, and that
you would not be here to-night.

Armand. Well, you see you were mistaken, for I *am* here.

Prudence. When did you arrive?

Armand. An hour ago.

Prudence. Have you seen Camille?

Armand. I have not.

Prudence. She will be here to-night.

Armand. Ah, indeed! Then perhaps I may see her.

Prudence. Perhaps you may see her! How strangely
you talk!

Armand. How would you have me talk?

Prudence. You are cured, then?

Armand. Oh, perfectly! Else why should I be *here*?

Prudence. So you have ceased to think of her?

Armand. No! I cannot say that; for it would be untrue. But I confess the souvenir is not a very flattering one to her, nor pleasant one to me.

Prudence. Oh! I really think she loved you then, and even loves you still—that is a little; but it was quite time she *did* leave you. Even the old Duke refused to contribute a sous unless the relation between you were sundered. She was forsaking her friends—wasting her means—and everything she possessed was being sold to pay her debts.

Armand. It is different now?

Prudence. Yes, *very* different!

Armand. All her debts are paid?

Prudence. Every one!

Armand. By the Count de Varville?

Prudence. Yes!

Armand. So much the better!

Prudence. And so I tell her. That is just what I think —and I am glad you have come to your senses, and think so too. Now everything goes well. Horses, carriage, jewels, are all returned; and the luxury in which she lives would make you wonder how she could stay so long in that cage in which she lived with you in the country.

Armand. She is in Paris, then?

Prudence. Yes! She will be here soon. I have never seen her as she is now. She is scarcely an hour at home— operas, balls, suppers—and as for sleep, that scarcely visits her any more. After she left you, she was three days confined to bed; and the moment she got well enough to be out again, her revelry began; and so she has kept it up at the expense of her health, and I may say, her *life*. For if she continues thus, it cannot last long. Even now she looks more like a statue than a living thing.

Armand. [*Seeing Gustave.*] Madam Duverney, here is

a friend to whom I would speak. Will you have the goodness to excuse me?

Prudence. Oh, certainly; for I must sit down, or I shall faint with hunger. I wish they would hurry up the supper.

[*Goes up.*]

Armand. [*Taking Gustave's hand.*] So you received my letter?

Gustave. I did—and am here.

Armand. You thought Camille loved me—did you not?

Gustave. I did—and do still think so.

Armand. Read. [*Gives a letter.*]

Gustave. Did Camille write that?

Armand. She did.

Gustave. When?

Armand. One month ago.

Gustave. And what was your reply?

Armand. What *could* it be? The blow was so sudden that I thought I should go mad. She will be here to-night with Count de Varville. I have come here to meet him.

Gustave. Armand, for heaven's sake, be calm! Reflect where you are. If, indeed, Camille be false, she is unworthy of your love—and ask yourself if injury from such as are assembled here to-night be worthy the resentment of a gentleman.

Armand. Gustave, you are an honest man. I may require to-night the service of a friend. May I count on yours?

Gustave. You may, sir; although I wish it were to serve you in a worthier cause.

Armand. For *your* sake. To me it is more than worthy—it is sacred. [*Points to letter.*] These words were penned by her; but never emanated from her heart. They are the echo of the sweet words that scorpion Count de Varville has been hissing in her ear. It is with *him* that I would speak. By my hopes in her which he has blasted—by the infamy he has labeled on her name—I have sworn to be avenged!

Prompter. [*Without.*] Mademoiselle Camille Gauthier and Count de Varville.

Armand. She is here.

ENTER CAMILLE AND VARVILLE.

Olimpe. How late you are.

Varville. We have only now returned from the opera.

Prudence. [*To Camille.*] How lovely you look, my child —are you well?

Camille. Oh, very well!

Prudence. Armand is here.

Camille. Armand! [*Turns and sees him. They bow coldly. He goes to card table.*] Oh! I was wrong to come to this ball to-night!

Prudence. Well, you would have to meet some day; and it may as well be soon as late.

Camille. Oh! how pale he is!

Varville. Camille, Monsieur Duval is here.

Camille. I know it.

Varville. Are you sure you did not know he would be here before you came?

Camille. Certain.

Varville. Then promise me you will not speak to him.

Camille. I cannot promise that. [*Goes to sofa.*]

Gustave. Good evening, Camille!

Camille. Gustave! Oh, how glad I am to see you! And Nichette — how is she?

Gustave. Very well!

Camille. But why are you here? This is not your custom.

Gustave. Nor was it yours of late, Camille. What is the matter?

Camille. Oh, Gustave, I am so unhappy! Leave me.

Gustave. Why have you come here?

Camille. *He* would have it so. But it is well; for each night passed thus shortens the number of my days.

Gustave. Camille, leave this place.

Camille. Wherefore?

Gustave. Because Armand——

Camille. I know he despises me.

Gustave. No! He loves you! He is not well. You see how pale he is. He is much excited. I know not what may yet transpire between him and Count de Varville.

Camille. A duel! You are right, Gustave. I will leave instantly.

Varville. Where are you going, Camille?

Camille. Count, I am not well. I pray you lead me hence.

Varville. I understand, Camille. You would retire because Monsieur Duval is here. While I appreciate your consideration, I cannot consent to be driven from the place in which he chooses to intrude his presence. Know that I neither respect nor fear him. For that reason, you are here, and here you shall remain! [*She sinks back on the sofa.*]

Olimpe. What was the opera to-night?

Varville. La Favorite!

Armand. The story of a woman who deceived her lover.

Gaston. A very common case.

Armand. Oh! but she loved him; or she said so—much the same thing!

Gaston. Quite the same. You can never tell when they do, or when they don't. Their words are all alike. Yet we, poor devils, trust them to the last; for, in spite of all experience, man is but man.

Armand. And woman is but *woman!*

Olimpe. Why, my dear Armand, what a frightful game you are playing?

Armand. Yes! I would test the proverb:—"Happy at cards, unhappy in love!"

Gaston. Then I must be fearfully lucky at cards; for a more unlucky devil at the game of hearts——

Armand. [*Interrupting him.*] Hearts? Diamonds! Play diamonds, if you will win women! My friends, I hope to make a fortune to-night. And when I shall have made it, I will go and live in the country.

4

Olimpe. Alone?

Armand. Oh, no! With one who accompanied me there before, and who left me because I was poor! But I have found the way to bring her back again. It is this! [*Throws gold coin up in the air.*] Gold! Gold! At its magic sound the truant bird will perch upon my hand!

Gustave. I pray you, sir, forbear! See, your words have made her ill.

Armand. Then why is her friend silent? That was his cue! But he shall speak! [*Turns to company.*] It is a very good story, by the way. I must relate it. It is quite romantic; for there is a nobleman in it—a great Count—very rich in *pocket;* but history does not record the extent of his *honor!*

Varville. [*Advancing.*] Sir!

Camille. Varville, if you provoke Monsieur Duval, never speak to me again. You know me!

Armand. [*To Varville.*] Did you speak to me, sir?

Varville. Yes, sir! I was about to say that the happy vein which your fortune has struck to-night tempts me to venture mine! Besides, having learned from you how I may catch the bird, perhaps you will instruct me how to keep it. I, too, would test the proverb. I propose to take a lesson.

Armand. Which I will endeavor to teach you.

Varville. I hold a hundred louis, sir.

Armand. Be it so. What side, sir?

Varville. The one you reject.

Armand. A hundred louis to the left!

Varville. A hundred louis to the right!

Armand. [*To Gaston.*] Hold the cards.

Gaston. To the right, four—to the left, nine. Armand has gained.

Varville. Two hundred louis, then!

Armand. As you please. Two hundred louis! But have a care; if the proverb says: "Happy at play, unhappy in love," it also says: "Unhappy in love, happy at play!"

Varville.   I have no fear, sir!

Gaston.   Again:—six—eight—Armand has gained.

Olimpe.   Good! So, Count, you must pay for the champagne. Let us to supper. It is time we were at table.

Armand.   Shall we continue the game?

Varville.   No—not for the present.

Armand.   I owe you a revenge; and I promise to pay it at whatever game it may please you to adopt. Till then, I will remain your debtor.

Varville.   It shall no longer burthen you. I accept your will to be released from the obligation, and shall await your payment at the earliest moment.

Olimpe.   [*Taking Armand's arm.*] You have been ill-humored all the night.

Armand.   It is over now; for I have won the game.

Exeunt Armand, Olimpe, Gustave, Gaston, and Company.

Varville.   [*To Camille.*] Come with me.

Camille.   I will join you presently. I would speak with Prudence.

Varville.   If in ten minutes you are not with us there, [*Pointing to supper room.*] I will return. You understand!

Camille.   Leave me. [Exit Varville. *To Prudence.*] Go find Armand, and entreat him to come to me. I must speak to him.

Prudence.   If he refuse——

Camille.   He will not. He will seize the opportunity to tell me how he hates me. [Exit Prudence.] What's to be done? I must continue to deceive him. I made a sacred promise to his father. It must not be broken. Oh, heaven! give me strength to keep it. But this duel! How to prevent it! Peril honor, life, for me! Oh! No, no, no! Rather let him hate—despise me! Oh! he is here!

Enter Armand.

Armand.   Madam, did you send for me?

Camille.   I did, Armand! I would speak with you.

Armand.   Speak! I listen.

Camille. I have a few words to say to you—not of the past——

Armand. Oh, no! Let that be buried in the shame that shrouds it.

Camille. Oh! do not crush me with reproach. See how I am bowed before you, pale trembling, supplicating. Listen to me without hate, and hear me without anger. Say that you will forget the past, and—give me your hand.

Armand. [*Rejecting her hand.*] Pardon me, Madam. If your business with me is at an end, I will retire.

Camille. Stay—I will not detain you long. Armand, you must leave Paris!

Armand. Leave Paris! And why, Madam?

Camille. Because the Count de Varville seeks to quarrel with you, and I wish you to avoid him. I alone am to blame, and I alone should suffer.

Armand. And it is thus you counsel me to play the *coward's* part, and *fly*—fly from Count de Varville! What other counsel could come from such a source?

Camille. Armand, by the memory of the woman whom you once loved—in the name of the pangs it cost her to destroy your faith—and in the name of her who smiled from heaven upon the act that saved her son from shame—even in her name—your mother's name—Armand Duval, I charge you leave me! Fly—fly—anywhere from here—from me—or you will make me h man!

Armand. I understand, Madam. You tremble for your lover—your wealthy Count—who holds your fortune in his hands. You shudder at the thought of the event which would rob you of his gold; or, perhaps, his title, which, no doubt, ere long you hope to wear.

Camille. I tremble for *your life!*

Armand. You tremble for my life! Oh, you jest! What is my life or death to you? Had you such a fear when you wrote that letter? [*Takes out letter and reads.*] "Armand, forget me. The Count has offered me his protection. I accept it; for I know he loves me." Love you! Oh, had he loved you, you would not have been *here* to-night. These were your words. That they did not kill me was no fault of yours—and that I am not dead, is because I *cannot* die until I am avenged; because I *will not* die until I see the words you have graven on my brain imprinted in the blood of him who wronged me! And should your life-strings crack to part with him, he shall not live; for I have sworn it!

Camille. Armand, you wrong him! De Varville is innocent of all that has occurred!

Armand. He loves you, madam! *That* is his crime—the sin that he must answer for!

Camille. Oh, could you but know his thoughts, they would tell you that I *hate* him!

Armand. Why are you *his?* Why *here*—the plaything of his vanity, the trophy of his gold?

Camille. Oh, heaven! Armand! No—no! this must not be. You may retire! I have no more to say. Do not ask me, for I cannot tell!

Armand. Then I will tell you! Because you are heartless, truthless, and make a sale of that which you call love to him who bids the highest! Because when you found a man who truly loved you, who devoted every thought and act to bless and guard you, you fled from him at the very moment you were mocking him with a sacrifice you had not the courage to make. Horses, house and jewels must be parted with, and all for love! Oh, no! that could not be! They must remain unsold, and so they did! They were returned, and with them, what? The bitter pangs of anguish and remorse which fill your breast, even while it heaves beneath a weight of gems!—the fixed despair which sits upon that brow on which those diamonds look down in mockery! And this is what the man you love has done for you! These are *his* triumphs—the wages of *your* shame!

Camille. Armand, you have pierced my heart—you have bowed me in the dust! Is it fit that you should die for such

a wretch as you have drawn? Is it fit that you should taint
your name in such a cause as hers? Remember those who
love you, Armand!—your sister, father, friends, Camille!
For her sake do not peril life and honor! Do not meet the
Count again! Quit Paris! Forget your wrongs for *my*
sake! See, at your feet I ask it in my name!

Armand. On condition that you fly from Paris with me!

Camille. Oh, you are mad!

Armand. I am indeed! I stand upon the brink of an
abyss, whence I must soar or fall! You can save me. A
moment since I thought I hated you. I tried to smother in
my breast the truth, that it was love—*love for you!* All
shall be forgotten—forgiven! We will fly from Paris and
the past! We will go to the end of the earth—away from
man—where not an eye shall feast a glance upon your form,
nor sound disturb your ear less gentle than the echoes which
repeat our tales of love!

Camille. This cannot be!

Armand. Again!

Camille. I would give a whole eternity of life to purchase
one short hour of bliss like that you've pictured now! But
it must not be! There is a gulf between us which I dare not
cross! I have sworn to forget you—to avoid you—to tear
you from my thoughts, though it should uproot my reason!

Armand. You have sworn to whom?

Camille. To one who had the right to ask me!

Armand. To the Count de Varville, who loves you! Now
say that you love *him*, and I will part with you forever!

Camille. [*Faltering.*] Yes, I love the Count de Varville!

Armand. [*Rushes to supper-room door, and violently
dashes it open.*] Enter all!

ALL THE CHARACTERS IN THE ACT RUSH IN.

Camille. What would you do?

Armand. You will see! [*To guests.*] You see that
woman?

Olimpe. Camille?

Armand. Yes! Camille Gauthier! Do you know what she has done?

All. No!

Armand. But you shall! She once sold her horses, carriage, diamonds—all to live with me, so much she loved me! This was generous—was it not? But what did I do? You shall hear! I accepted this sacrifice at her hands without repaying her! But it is not too late! I have repented—and now that I am rich, I am come to pay it back! You all bear witness that I have paid that woman, and that I owe her nothing!

[*He throws a shower of notes and gold upon Camille, who has thrown herself at his feet. De Varville advances suddenly and strikes him.*]

Varville. 'Tis false! You owe me revenge!

END OF ACT.

ACT FIFTH.

.SCENE:—*A poorly furnished chamber.*

CAMILLE *discovered asleep on a couch, and* GASTON *on a chair.*

Gaston [*Waking.*] I verily believe I have had a nap. I wonder if she wanted anything. No, she sleeps. What time is it? [*Looks at clock.*] Eight o'clock. I wish this room would stand still a moment. There's something the matter with my head. Ugh! ugh! ugh! It is very cold. Stay, she must be cold too. I thought there was a fire in this room when I lay down. Oh! here it is. [*Fixes fire.*]

Camille. Nanine, are you there?

Gaston. Yes! here I am.

Camille. Who is that?

Gaston. Gaston. It is only Gaston.

Camille. You frighten me. How came you here?

Gaston. [*Giving a cup of tea.*] Drink, first, and then you shall know all about it. Is it sweet enough?

Camille. Yes, Gaston, just as I like it.

Gaston. I thought so. I begin to think that nature intended me for a nurse.

Camille. What have you done with Nanine?

Gaston. Sent her to bed. When I came here two hours ago, I found a man at the door giving her a little of his mind upon the matter of some accounts that were standing against her on his bread bill. I did not exactly like the manner in which he expressed himself, and so I told him. Whereupon he chose to direct his conversation to me. Handing him the amount of his claim, I was just in the act of handing him out at the window, when it suddenly occurred to me that the noise might wake you; so I ended the affair by giving him a gentle impetus, which sent him down stairs upon an improved plan of speed.

Camille. But Nanine—

Gaston. Well, the poor girl looked worn-out with fatigue. She could scarcely keep her eyes open. I told her to go to bed. I entered here. You were fast asleep. I placed myself on that sofa near the fire, listened to the ticking of the clock until I fancied I was back waltzing in the ball-room I had just left; and when I awoke just now, such a turning round as this little room kept up! Then I must trim the fire, and make a noise, and wake you. That was too bad. But I always was an awkward fellow.

Camille. Oh, you are so good to come and stay with me. But you must be fatigued.

Gaston. Fatigued! Ha! ha! Well, I think when I give all my nights to balls and masques, it would be hard if I could not spare an hour of the morning to watch a poor sick girl; eh! Camille? But how are you to-day? You have not told me yet.

Camille. I feel much better. When Nanine awakes, I think I shall get up.

Gaston. Good! [ENTER NANINE.] And here she is. So I will just get my coat that I left in the entry, and be with you in a moment. There, Nanine, get her up.

EXIT GASTON. *Nanine helps Camille.*

Camille. Poor girl! You must be very tired.

Nanine. No, Madam; I could never tire in your service. [*Camille kisses her.*] Oh thank you, Madam.

Camille. Nanine, you have been a faithful friend.

Nanine. Oh, Madam, I never can forget that I was once an orphan, without a friend or a home, and that I found both in your care.

Gaston. [ENTERING.] Here we are. Why I declare, my little patient looks well to-day—all the result of my nursing. But here, you want a pillow, don't you? [*Places a pillow for her head.*] Now we are all right. [EXIT NANINE.]

Camille. How can I ever repay such kindness?

Gaston. By forgetting that you owe it. Let us talk of something else. It is a beautiful day. You have slept well all night. In an hour or two the sun will be high. I will come for you in a carriage, wrap you up in shawls—we will take a long drive—I shall get you a little bird—you shall eat it on your return—then you shall scold me for making you so tired—you will lay your head down softly on your pillow and sleep till morning. Will that do?

Camille. Do you think I will be strong enough?

Gaston. To be sure you will. Besides am I not your nurse? You must obey your nurse, you know. And now I will go and see my mother. It has been fifteen days since she laid eyes on me. She will give me a reception! Ah, I am a bad boy, Camille, and dont deserve to have so good a mother.

Camille. If she but knew your heart.

Gaston. Yes! I think myself that little machine called heart, would not work so badly if it were properly managed. Good-bye! Oh, Camille, do you want your key? That is, would you require it? The key of that little drawer, I mean.

Camille. No, there is nothing in it.

Gaston. That was just what I thought; and so I locked

it, lest it might get out. You will find the key in that little box on top there, should you want it before I return. Good-bye!

Camille. Stay! What have you done? You have filled my little purse. Is it not so?

Gaston. Never mind; we will talk of that again. Camille, why was it empty? Why did I find you here this morning in suffering and in want?

Camille. What could I do?

Gaston. You could have sent to me.

Camille. You, on whom I never bestowed the favor of a smile, scarcely a kind word.

Gaston. And what of that? I am sure I deserved worse than that; for I know I was a great fool. Olimpe could tell you that. She knows it. But never mind. You must let me be your brother, and I will come here every day and nurse you until you get well. Do you know, Camille, I have grown tired of the first edition of my life. I think I will issue a second, revised and corrected, with notes by the author, and see how it will look in new type. What do you think of it?

Camille. I think well of it, Gaston; and so will your mother. Ask her counsel—tell her your wish—and she will help you to it. Make *her* love the altar of your truth, and it will rise before you as a pillar of fire to guide you in adversity.

Gaston. I will go to her now, and tell her what you say. You will be ready in an hour.

Camille. Yes, good-bye. Remember all that I have said.

Gaston. It shall lie upon my heart like a prayer.

[EXIT.

Camille. I remember the time I used to laugh at him. Where is the crowd who smiled upon me then? And he is here.

ENTER NANINE

Nanine. Madam, here are some presents, I am sure.

Camille. Presents? Oh, I remember, it is new-years day. The last brought many changes. This day twelve-month! Ah, Nanine, those days are gone.

Nanine. Would you not like to see what these contain, madam?

Camille. Yes, let me see. A ring, with Gaston's card. Bless him! Oh, he is so good to think of me. A bracelet from the dear old Duke. He does not know that I am ill. Ah, if he knew how changed I am, he would forgive me. Bonbons from Nichette and Gustave. The world has a better memory than I gave it credit for. What is this? A letter from Nichette. [*Reads.*] "My dear Camille:—I have called twenty times, but I have never been permitted to see you. I hope you are very well. I wish you a happy new-year; for it is the happiest of my life. It is my wedding-day. Gustave and I desire you will be present at the ceremony. It is all we want to make our joy complete. Do pray come. The ceremony will take place at ten o'clock, at the church St. Madeleine. Believe me, your very happy and devoted friend, Nichette." It is her wedding-day. This day brings happiness to all but me. Here, Nanine, let me have a pen and paper. [*Writes.*] There now, send that letter to the church St. Madeleine, and tell the bearer not to hand it to Nichette until after the ceremony of her marriage. You understand?

Nanine. Yes, madam.

Camille. Some one rang. Open the door.

NANINE EXITS, *and immediately* RE-ENTERS.

Nanine. It is Madam Duverney. She says she must see you.

Camille. Then let her enter.

Prudence. [ENTERING.] Well, my dear Camille, how are you this morning?

Camille. Better, I thank you.

Prudence. My dear Camille, will you have the goodness to send Nanine out of the room a moment? I would speak to you alone.

Camille. Nanine, you can take that letter to the Madeleine yourself, if you wish. You have need of a little air.

Nanine. But, madam, I do not like to leave you alone.

Camille. Prudence will remain with me till you return.

Nanine. Yes, madam. [EXIT.

Prudence. [*Aside.*] That girl watches me when I enter this room as if I were a thief. Well, my dear Camille, I have a favor to ask of you.

Camille. What is it?

Prudence. Have you any money about you, dear?

Camille. Money! Where could I get it? The last money that I saw was in your hands. Nanine obtained it on the last jewel I possessed. She gave it all to you. I have not seen you since.

Prudence. I know, dear; but I have had such trouble. I thought Olimpe could oblige me; but she is as badly off as I am. You know she ran off with that man, because she thought he was rich. Well, it turns out that he is as poor as a church mouse. So here she is, back in Paris, without a friend or a sous. She sent me to Gaston this morning, begging him to forgive her, and to take her back. But, oh, dear! if you had seen him when I gave him her letter!

Camille. Have you seen him this morning?

Prudence. Not five minutes since. I saw him at the ball last night. He said he was going to breakfast with his mother. So I went there and found him.

Camille. What did he say?

Prudence. Oh, dear, don't ask me! He even showed the letter to his mother, and then threw it in the fire. And then she kissed him. I really don't know what to say to Olimpe; for as sure as I am sitting here he seemed to cry for very joy that he was rid of her, or something else, I cannot say.

Camille. Oh, he is with his mother! I am happy.

Prudence. Yes, I don't know what Olimpe will do; for though she did not love him, he was very convenient. Poor girl! this will not be a very happy day for her. We can spend it together; for I assure you I have only got five francs in the world.

Camille. Three hours ago I had not *one*. How much do you want?

Prudence. Unfortunately I invited some friends to a supper to-night. Besides some other expenses that always come with new-years day, you know. Yes, I think two hundred francs would cover it all. You couldn't lend me that little sum until the end of the month, could you, dear?

Camille. The end of the month! I shall not need it then. Count that. [*Takes purse which Gaston placed in Casket, and gives it to her.*]

Prudence. Oh, dear! what a pity you are not well, Camille. We could all come and dine with you to-day; then you would join our supper in the evening, and we could have such a delightful time!

Camille. How much is there?

Prudence. [*Counting.*] Five hundred francs I should say.

Camille. Take of it what you require.

Prudence. Have you enough without this, dear? [*Puts purse in her pocket.*] Perhaps I am robbing you?

Camille. Never mind me, I have all that I shall want.

Prudence. Oh, thank you! You have rendered me a great service. Now I'll leave you. I will call to-morrow and see how you are. Oh, you are looking better to-day, indeed you are. Now that the fine weather is come, the country air would do you good.

Camille. See if Nanine be there.

Prudence. I will, dear! Good-bye, and thank you, again. Perhaps I will call in this evening. You will not feel lonely until Nanine returns,—will you, dear?

Camille. Oh no,—you may go.

Prudence. That's a dear; for I have some purchases to make. Then I must go to bed; for I can scarcely keep my eyes open. [EXIT.

Camille. And that was one of my friends! Oh, what is death compared to life like that? [*Takes out a letter and*

reads.] "Madam: I have learned of the duel which has
" taken place between Armand and the Count de Varville—
" not from my son; for he has quitted France without even
" saying adieu to me; but from the Count de Varville, who,
" thanks to heaven, is out of danger, and has told me all.
" You have kept your oath, and proved how well you love.
" I have this day written to Armand, avowing all: that it
" was I who forced you to destroy his peace. He is far
" away; but he will soon return. Be of good cheer.
" It is Armand's father speaks to you. Believe me your
" friend: George Duval. November 15th." Six weeks
have passed since I received this letter, and though I
know it word for word, the hour scarcely passes that I do
not read it over in hopes to glean from it new life and
courage. If I could but hear from *him!* If I could but live
till Spring! I will! I must, yes, I must see him before
I die! [*Looks in the glass.*] Oh! how changed I am!
However the doctor says that he will cure me! Yes! Yes!
I must have patience! Spring will soon be here, and I
do so love the Spring! No frown upon *her* brow forbids
the humblest flower to hope. She smiles on all alike,—the
camelia and the cowslip, the daisy and the rose! May I not
hope that she will smile on me? I wish Nanine were come.
It is the first day of the year,—the day that brings new life
to every heart. Oh, if Armand were only here, I am sure
I would be saved. Yes! Yes! he will soon be here,—and
so I must be well! [*Opens window and looks out.*] Oh,
how bright and beautiful every thing appears! And there's
a darling little child! See how it skips along with an
armful of toys! And now it laughs and looks up here as
though it wished to give me one. Oh, how I would like to
kiss it!

Nanine. [ENTERING *hurriedly.*] Oh, Madam, are you up?
Camille. Yes, Nanine! did you give the letter?
Nanine. Yes, Madam! And then I ran back all the way;
for oh!—but are you sure you are well enough to hear—I
mean to sit up?

Camille. Oh, you see how well I am. Prudence left me long ago, and I walked over here myself. Am I not grown strong?

Nanine. But you must promise me to keep perfectly calm.

Camille. What's the matter? Something has happened.

Nanine. Yes, Madam! And I ran all the way to tell you. But don't be frightened; for a sudden joy awaits you!

Camille. A joy, say you? *Aye! speak to me of joy!* You have seen Armand! He is come! Armand, come—come! Oh, where are you? [ENTER ARMAND.] Armand, you are come; but it is too late!

Armand. Oh, Camille! You must not speak of death, but life! Live, oh! live for me!

Camille. Armand, it is wise—it is well—it is *just!* I have been guilty. Living, the memory of that guilt would haunt me like a spectre! It would flit between me and your smile! It would stand upon the platform of the past, growing monstrous, hideous with my years, darkening with its fearful shadow my passage to the close! Death's kindly veil will hide it from my sight—the world will bury its resentment in my grave, and remembering my sufferings may forget my faults!

Armand. Camille, *you* were *my* world! With you I had all things—without you nothing!

Camille. Closer, closer, Armand, and listen while I speak! Armand, keep this. [*Giving likeness.*] I had it taken for you long ago. You will gaze upon it often, I am sure, and think of me. And if some day, a lovely, pure, chaste girl, should seek your love, I ask you in my name, to listen to her kindly and let her lay her heart upon the shrine which once was mine. And if she ask you who this was,—tell her. Say it was a young friend who loved you well, and who from her peaceful home beyond the sky keeps vigil with the stars, shedding smiles upon you both! If this silent image cost her heart one pang, bury it in my grave, without remorse, without a tear!

Armand. Oh! Camille! Camille! Hope smiles no more for me!

Camille. Armand, the day I met your father, I wore upon my breast these little flowers, the same you gave me in the morning. When I left you that evening and came to Paris, I took the flowers and kissed them; but they were withered, bloomless, faded—and with them every little hope that blossomed on my heart! I have kept them ever since. [*Takes flowers from casket.*] See how pale and blighted they have grown. They are called "Heart's-ease"—a pretty name! Armand, keep them. They will remind you how I loved you— and, when I am dead, plant others like them on the grave where I shall sleep in peace.

ENTER NANINE, NICHETTE, GUSTAVE, AND GASTON.

Armand. Gustave, this is a bitter hour!

Nichette. Oh, Camille! how you frightened me! You wrote me you were dying!

Camille. And so I am, Nichette! But I can smile; for I am happy! You, too, are happy. You are a bride. You will think of me sometimes,—will you not? And Gustave, too,—you will speak of me together! Armand, come! Your hand! You must not leave me! Armand here, and all my friends! Oh, this is happiness! And Gaston, too! I am so glad you are come! Armand is here, and I am so happy! Oh, how strange!

Armand. What is it, Camille?

Camille. All the pain is gone! Is this life? Now everything appears to change. Oh, how beautiful! Do not wake me—I am so sleepy! [*Dies.*

Armand. Camille! Camille! Camille! Dead! Dead!

Nichette. Sleep in peace, Camille. Thou hast loved much, —much shall be forgiven thee.

END.

In the Cemetery MONTMARTRE, in Paris, rests the body of her upon whose melancholy history this play is founded. About the grave, many flowers, planted by the hand of some kind friend, continue to bloom in beauty. An humble tombstone bears the following inscription:

HERE REPOSES

ALPHONSINE PLESSUS,

Born, Jan. 15, 1824.
Died, Feb. 3, 1847.